Dedicated to my son,

Charles Mikhail Wagner,

who has shown me unconditional love.

www.mascotbooks.com

Mickey on the Move

For more information, please contact:
Mascot Books
620 Herndon Parkway, Suite 320
Herndon, VA 20170
info@mascotbooks.com

Library of Congress Control Number: 2020909275

CPSIA Code: PRT0920A
ISBN-13: 978-1-64543-344-6

Printed in the United States

Mickey
on the Move

Michelle Wagner

Illustrated by
Jenny Phelps

The neighborhood was noisy as everyone got ready for the first day of the new school year. Kids ran around looking for lost sneakers and backpacks and books. Their parents scrambled after them, warning them not to be late or to leave anything behind. Lazy summer mornings were all over now! Just one house on the block was nice and calm...

Mickey and his mom sat down and had breakfast together and reviewed the plan one last time. His mom had already talked to all of the teachers and staff—even the principal—to arrange Mickey's classes and schedule. Even though Mickey was starting sixth grade at a big new school, he wasn't worried. After all, this was the fifth new school he'd started—Mickey was used to being on the move!

Gathering his backpack, Mickey climbed on his trusty bike. He was excited to pedal over the two short blocks to his new school.

His mom used to have to drive him all over the place, for hours and hours each day, just to go to school.

For a little bit, she even went with him!

They sat in the classroom together and learned American Sign Language and practiced speaking.

ickey doesn't hear things the same way that most of his friends do. His mom realized when he was very young that he couldn't hear at all. Though many people who are deaf or have a hard time hearing can use hearing aids to make everything louder, those didn't help Mickey. Mickey and his mom visited many doctors and experts, and before he even turned three years old, he had surgery on his ears.

The doctors gave him bilateral cochlear implants, which are tiny electronic devices that send signals directly to the parts of the brain in charge of hearing.

When Mickey arrived at his brand-new school, his friend Lola was already waiting outside for him.

Mickey and Lola are in the sixth grade together and they have known each other their whole lives. When other kids and teachers need to pay closer attention to what Mickey is saying, Lola always helps out. She's a great friend!

For some classes, Mickey spends more time with a teacher in a quieter room. That way he can concentrate harder on things like reading, math, and speech.

He spends most of his day in the classroom with Lola and the rest of the kids. His teacher wears a special microphone that is connected with Mickey's cochlear implants so he can understand everything.

Mickey is very creative, and his favorite class is art. He loves drawing and painting pictures of his trusty bike, as well as cars and motorcycles. Mickey wants to be a police officer someday so that he can drive around and help people. He knows he'll always be on the move!

**W**hen Mickey rides his bike home at the end of his first day, his mom is excited to hear about how well everything went.

For the whole first week, Mickey shares his school stories with her each day as they travel from soccer practice to tennis and swimming.

Everything seems great, so Mickey's mom is surprised when she gets a call a few days later from Mickey's teacher.

Mickey's been sneaking into the library for lunch!

Mickey's mom is puzzled. She knows Mickey is happy in class and at home and that he has great friends—why

Aha!

"The cafeteria—is it very noisy?" Mickey's mom asks.

"Well, there are a lot of kids buzzing around, getting meals and talking to each other," Mickey's teacher says thoughtfully.

"That explains it," Mickey's mom replies. "Since Mickey's cochlear implants don't distinguish sounds the exact same way as most people's ears, noisy places are much harder to deal with."

"Yes, that makes sense. But no one can eat in the library!" Mickey's teacher cries.

"The school is big, but so is the whole world," Mickey's mom says. "Everyone needs a little extra planning to make sure they have everything they need to be happy and healthy."

Mickey's mom, his teacher, and his friends all sit down and help Mickey brainstorm a solution.

The next day, Mickey and Lola and all of their friends find a quieter table tucked away where they can all enjoy lunch and have conversations with each other.

When they're all done eating, they're all on the move together—they have special permission to go to the library for an even quieter space to have fun.

The End!

About the Author

Born and raised in Chicago, Michelle (Miata) Wagner was always a very positive and outgoing woman. Her energetic love for children and zest for life is admired by everyone who knows her. After discovering her adopted son was profoundly deaf in both ears, she made it her mission to get him what he needed to live his best life. After Mickey's bilateral cochlear implant surgery, the journey truly began. Together, Michelle and her son Mickey went for years of extensive private speech lessons in different locations and attended specialized schools far from their home, allowing Mickey to progress and be mainstreamed with individualized help at the school in his town, St. Helena. Michelle is a realtor whose career background involves restaurants and always helping other people. She has dedicated time and support to charities and events to help other children with hearing loss, and helps families work through the different approaches of raising a special needs child in a typical environment. Today, Mickey is thriving at school and is social with his friends. Michelle coaches his soccer team and makes sure that Mickey has the courage to be his optimal self.